Xtreme Adventure

STORM CHASING

BY S.L. HAMILTON

EDGE
FRANKLIN WATTS

LONDON•SYDNEY

First published in Great Britain in 2015 by The Watts Publishing Group

First published in the USA by ABDO Publishing Company.

Editor: John Hamilton
Graphic Design: Sue Hamilton
Cover Design: Sue Hamilton

Acknowledgements:
Cover Photo: Corbis
Interior Photos: Alamy-pgs 20-21; AP-pgs 1, 2-3 & 8-9; Corbis-pgs 17, 24-25 & 26-27;
Defense Video & Imagery Distribution System-pgs 10, 11, 22 (inset) & 32; Getty-pgs
4-5, 6-7, 12-13, 14 (inset), 14-15, 18-19 & 28-29; Midland-pg 6 (inset); National
Oceanic and Atmospheric Administration-pgs 16, 22-23 & 23 (inset top); U.S. Air
Force-pg 23 (inset bottom).

Dewey number 551.5'5
HB ISBN 978 1 4451 4033 9
Library ebook ISBN 978 1 4451 4036 0

Printed in China

Franklin Watts
An imprint of
Hachette Children's Group
Part of The Watts Publishing Group
Carmelite House
50 Victoria Embankment
London EC4Y 0DZ

An Hachette UK Company
www.hachette.co.uk

www.franklinwatts.co.uk

CONTENTS

STORM CHASING

While other people race inside, storm chasers head out into the wildest weather on the planet. They are brave, fearless and bold. Professionals love the thrills and adventure of their work. But they also know and respect nature's fury.

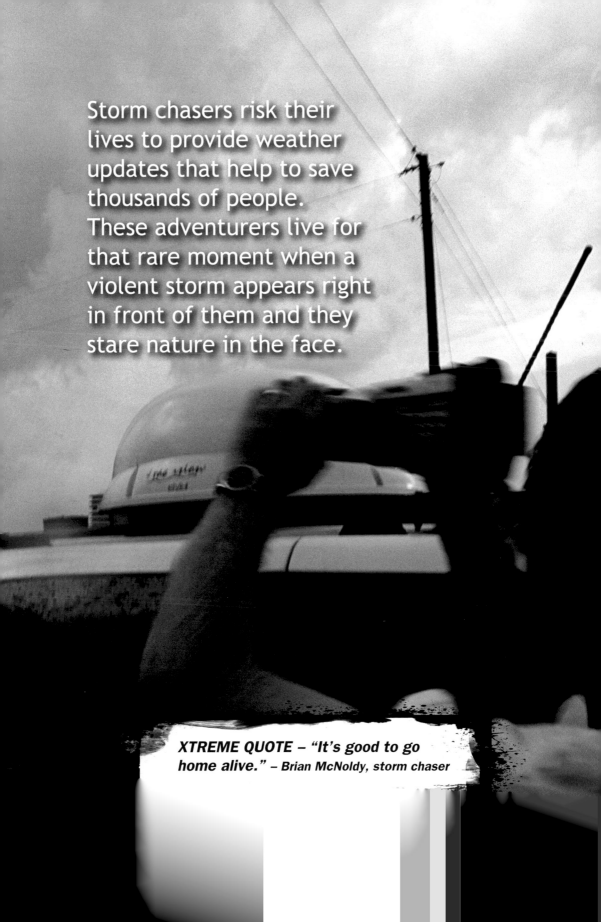

Storm chasers risk their lives to provide weather updates that help to save thousands of people. These adventurers live for that rare moment when a violent storm appears right in front of them and they stare nature in the face.

XTREME QUOTE – *"It's good to go home alive."* – *Brian McNoldy, storm chaser*

TOOLS & EQUIPMENT

Many storm chasers find storms using portable weather stations which include radar. Many have NOAA (National Oceanic and Atmospheric Administration) weather radios that give constant weather updates.

A sturdy, four-wheel-drive vehicle provides transportation over rough roads. Maps and GPS equipment help locate the quickest way to a developing storm.

XTREME FACT– *Some professional tornado chasers protect themselves inside a Tornado Intercept Vehicle (TIV). This is a heavy armoured vehicle (shown left). A few TIVs are strong enough to allow chasers to get inside a tornado.*

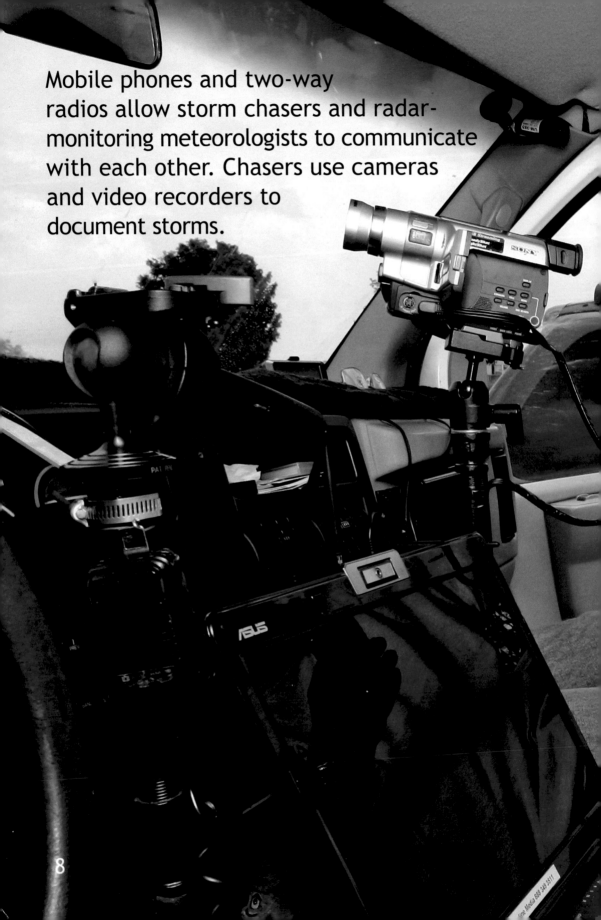

Mobile phones and two-way radios allow storm chasers and radar-monitoring meteorologists to communicate with each other. Chasers use cameras and video recorders to document storms.

XTREME FACT – Storm chasers are often 'first responders' – the first people at the scene following a violent storm. They travel with emergency first-aid supplies.

DANGERS

High winds, hail, lightning strikes, flying debris, flooding and inattentive drivers are all constant dangers for storm chasers. Even experienced storm chasers can be surprised by tornadoes that are hidden behind thick walls of rain. Their vehicles can be picked up and overturned by tornadoes.

A wrecked car overturned by a tornado in Henryville, Indiana, USA.

A tornado-driven piece of debris impales a car seat.

Storm chasers face powerful winds that can turn broken branches and other debris into killer projectiles. Adventurers must also protect themselves from blasting hail as large as cricket balls.

Storm chasers also face other dangers on the road. Many people have been killed in car accidents during a storm chase. Drivers sometimes talk on the phone or look out of the window at the growing storm instead of watching the road.

XTREME FACT – Professional storm chasers Carl Young, Tim Samaras and his son, Paul, were killed in Oklahoma, USA in 2013. They were following a massive tornado. It lifted their car off the road. They were unable to escape.

Drivers who cannot see properly because of heavy rain and hail are also a threat. There is also the danger of people fleeing the area. They are frightened and may be driving too fast.

If there are a lot of chasers out on the road it can be very difficult to escape danger if a tornado suddenly changes direction.

CHASING TORNADOES

Many professional storm chasers go after tornadoes trying to learn more about how the storms form and how they dissipate. Some storm chasers are developing new ways to send earlier tornado warnings.

Scientists place equipment in front of an oncoming tornado in Wyoming, USA.

A scientific instrument measures the wind speed and direction of an oncoming tornado.

Professional storm chasers are often trained meteorologists or atmospheric scientists. Long-time amateur storm chasers also know the warning signs of a possible tornado. Both professional and amateur storm chasers give local radio and TV stations up-to-the-minute information about severe weather conditions.

A Doppler on Wheels (DOW) portable weather radar vehicle owned by the Center for Severe Weather Research is used by scientists to gather information about a nearby tornado.

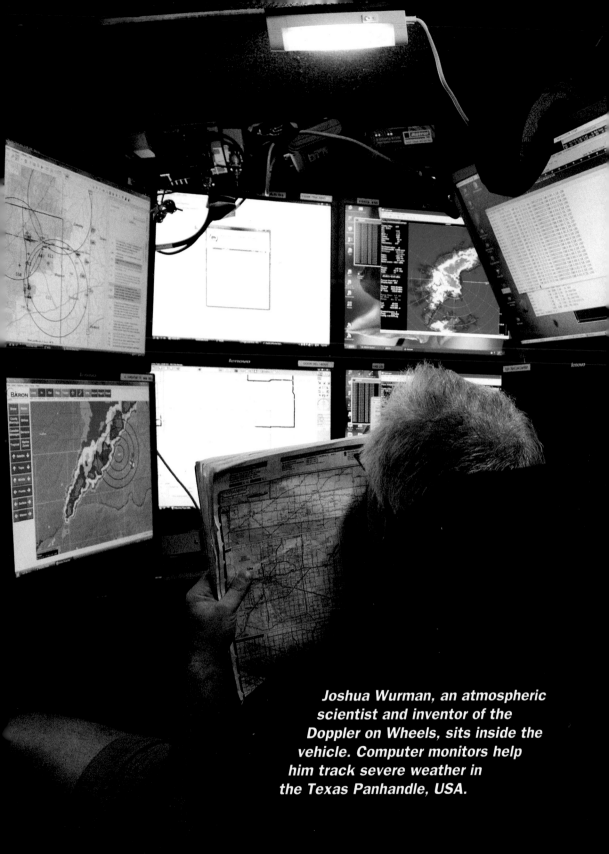

Joshua Wurman, an atmospheric scientist and inventor of the Doppler on Wheels, sits inside the vehicle. Computer monitors help him track severe weather in the Texas Panhandle, USA.

Some adventurers travel with professional storm chasers on tours. These weather fans help the professionals track developing severe storms while learning how to stay safe in dangerous conditions.

Some inexperienced storm chasers put themselves in harm's way by getting too close to violent storms. They yearn for the excitement of chasing down a tornado. Some pay for the opportunity with their lives.

Members of Tempest Tours hurry to take their last photos after being asked to return to their waiting van as a tornado approaches.

19

CHASING WATERSPOUTS

A waterspout is a
tornado that forms
over warm water.
Waterspouts are
dangerous to people
and ships. They
may make landfall,
and bring strong
winds and damaging
rain. Storm chasers
warn people
near shorelines
about incoming
waterspouts.

Storm chasers in a helicopter watch the intensity and direction of a waterspout near the Florida Keys, USA.

CHASING HURRICANES

Hurricanes form over the warm waters of the tropics. Hurricane chasers are more likely to be in the air than on the ground.

U.S. AIR FORCE

NOAA Hurricane Hunters

NOAA and the US Air Force have trained 'Hurricane Hunters'. These government personnel fly heavy aircraft with special instrumentation directly into hurricanes. Winds there reach spiraling speeds of more than 119 kph. On board, meteorologists and pilots use training and technology to gather scientific information, as well as help forecast a hurricane's path.

Once a hurricane hits shore, storm chasers on land track the storm's wind speed and path. They note storm surges — the sudden rise of ocean water to greater-than-normal heights that flow inland. Warnings are important.

24

In 2005, Hurricane Katrina hit the coastal areas of Florida, Louisiana, Mississippi, and Texas in the USA. It was the United States's costliest natural disaster and one of the five most deadly hurricanes, with 1,836 people killed.

Chasing Thunderstorms

Thunderstorms are amazing weather events. However, they are also deadly. Lightning, hail, flooding and hidden tornadoes are all threats found within severe thunderstorms. Storm chasers who go after thunderstorms for weather information, photos or just adventure must be extremely careful.

XTREME FACT – Lightning kills approximately 15,000 people worldwide each year.

Small radios can warn thunderstorm chasers that a lightning strike is about to happen. The electromagnetic charge between the clouds and the ground can be heard on a radio as a loud, intense crackling noise. This warning tells storm chasers to get back to their vehicles or to a safe building.

XTREME FACT – Chasers follow the 30:30 rule: after seeing lightning, if you can't count to 30 before hearing thunder, get inside immediately. Don't leave until 30 minutes after the last clap of thunder.

Storm chasers see amazing sights and have extreme adventures. The most successful ones know how to protect themselves while helping people and gaining knowledge.

GLOSSARY

ATMOSPHERIC SCIENTIST
A person who studies all areas of Earth's atmosphere, including weather and climate.

DISSIPATE
To dissapear, such as when a storm fades.

DOPPLER RADAR
A special radar system that uses the Doppler effect to measure the location, speed and intensity of a storm.

GPS (GLOBAL POSITIONING SYSTEM)
A system of orbiting satellites that transmits information to GPS receivers on Earth. Using information from the satellites, receivers can calculate location, speed, and direction with great accuracy.

METEOROLOGIST
A person who studies and predicts the weather.

National Oceanic and Atmospheric Administration
NOAA is a United States organisation that researches and collects data about the world's atmosphere and oceans and the creatures that live there.

Radar
Radar stands for <u>ra</u>dio <u>d</u>etection <u>an</u>d <u>r</u>anging. It is a way to detect objects using special radio waves. Radar can tell operators how big an object is, how fast it is moving, its altitude and its direction.

Storm Surge
When ocean waters suddenly rise to much greater-than-normal heights and flow far inland. A storm surge is usually caused by a hurricane's winds pushing on the ocean's surface.

INDEX